Y0-DLU-173

PRINCESS PROTECTION PROGRAM

Top Secret TIARAS

By Wendy Loggia

Based on "Princess Protection Program," Teleplay by Annie DeYoung

Based on the Story by David Morgasen and Annie DeYoung

New York

visit us at www.abdopublishing.com

Reinforced library bound edition published in 2011 by Spotlight, a division of ABDO Group, 8000 West 78th Street, Edina, Minnesota 55439. This edition reprinted by arrangement with Disney Press, an imprint of Disney Book Group, LLC. www.disneybooks.com

Printed in the United States of America, Melrose Park, Illinois.
042010
092010
This book contains at least 10% recycled materials.

Copyright © 2009 by Disney Enterprises, Inc. All rights reserved. Original book published by Disney Press, an imprint of Disney Book Group. No part of this book may be reproduced or transmitted in any form or by any means, electronic or mechanical, including photocopying, recording, or by any information storage and retrieval system, without written permission from the publisher. For information address:
Disney Press, 44 S. Broadway 10th Floor, White Plains, NY 10601.

Library of Congress Cataloging-in-Publication Data
This title was previously cataloged with the following information:

Loggia, Wendy.
Top secret tiaras / Adapted by Wendy Loggia.
 p. cm. (Princess Protection Program ; #3)
 I. Title. II. Series: Princess Protection Program.

[Fic]--dc22   2009926913

ISBN 978-1-59961-745-9 (reinforced library edition)

Spotlight

All Spotlight books have reinforced library binding and are manufactured in the United States of America.

Chapter 1

*R*osie stared at her laptop screen, holding her breath. Come on, come on . . . she thought.

She was in the middle of filling out an application for the event she'd been waiting forever to attend: the Princess Summit. Every four years, royal families from around the world sent their daughters to the summit to begin their training in diplomacy and to meet other girls who wore diamond-encrusted tiaras. Rosie had looked forward to being one of them since she was a little princess.

Except there was the problem. Rosie

wasn't a princess anymore. She was Queen Rosalinda Marie Montoya Fiore of the principality of Costa Luna—a sixteen-year-old head of state. Her mother had been a peasant who'd married into royalty. After the king died, the throne had passed directly to the only person entitled to be queen—Rosie.

And were queens allowed to attend the Princess Summit?

In a brief moment of panic, Rosie had a notion that maybe she could try to go incognito. After all, she had passed as a regular teen once before—as Rosie González in Lake Monroe, Louisiana. If she wasn't allowed to attend the summit as herself, maybe she could pretend to be someone else. A princess no one had ever heard of.

But that would be crazy, Rosie thought with a sigh, twirling a strand of her long dark hair around her finger. Not to mention wrong. The whole point of the summit was to bring young royals together from around the world and encourage a deeper understanding among the attending nations. There was no way she could go as anyone but Queen Rosalinda. And that's why she had stopped filling out the application and IM'd the coordinator of the summit to find out if she was eligible to attend.

Rosie glanced around the royal office—her office. It had once been her father's, and Rosie had fond memories of him sitting at his desk, signing royal decrees, making phone calls, and conducting important meetings. But the king had always had time for her. Once he had interrupted a gathering of ambassadors to let a six-year-old Rosie proudly show off her latest masterpiece—a finger painting of the bright pink flowers outside his office.

And they're still just as pretty, Rosie thought with a smile as she gazed out the huge windows. Her mother, Sophia, had insisted they redecorate the office now that it was Rosie's, and the room was a beautiful blend of everything Rosie loved—lilac-colored walls, comfortable slipcovered sofas, a beautiful antique desk that had belonged to her grandmother, and her favorite pictures framed on the wall.

It was a room fit for a princess . . . and a queen.

Rosie's laptop chimed with an IM.

PrincessSummitHQ: Good morning, Your Highness. I apologize for the delay. The crown princess of Harguay was having difficulty downloading the application.

HRHQueenRosalinda: Your apology is unnecessary, but accepted.

PrincessSummitHQ: Your Highness is without question eligible to attend the Princess Summit. It is for young royals—as long as one meets the age requirements and falls between the ages of fifteen and twenty-two, princesses and queens are both welcome.

"Yes!" Rosie shouted, spinning around in her velvet-upholstered desk chair.

HRHQueenRosalinda: That is wonderful news. Thank you!

PrincessSummitHQ: And, Your Highness, because you are a head of state, we invite you to bring a personal assistant or lady-in-waiting. We appreciate how busy your schedule is and understand the need for our royal leaders to have their own attendants.

Rosie paused. She didn't have a lady-in-waiting. But she did have a best friend who didn't have any spring-break plans. . . .

HRHQUEENROSALINDA: OH, THAT SOUNDS WONDERFUL! THANK YOU AGAIN.

PRINCESSSUMMITHQ: YOUR HIGHNESS? ONE MORE THING THAT WE WOULD LIKE TO MENTION, AS IT HAS CAUSED A CONSIDERABLE AMOUNT OF INTEREST AMONG THE OTHER ATTENDING PRINCESSES. THIS YEAR, WE ARE OPENING UP THE SUMMIT NOT ONLY TO PRINCESSES AND QUEENS, BUT TO PRINCES AND KINGS AS WELL.

Rosie's mind was whirling as she signed off. Princes and kings? She couldn't think of any kings off the top of her head who fell within the age requirements, but there were definitely a number of eligible princes.

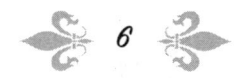

"I wonder if Prince Darius will be there," she mused aloud, leaning back in her seat and curling her legs underneath her. He was an old family friend, and Rosie hadn't seen him in quite some time. It would be nice to be able to catch up with him.

Speaking of catching up, Rosie picked up her cell and speed-dialed someone she couldn't wait to share the good news with.

Her best friend, Carter Mason.

Carter hopped up from her perch behind the cash register at Joe's Bait Shack faster than you could say night crawlers and ran outside, clutching her cell phone.

"Dad!" she called, waving frantically to her father as he hosed off muddy canoes in the boat-rental area. "We need to talk!"

"You look like a girl who just found out she's going on a trip next week with her best friend," Mr. Mason said, his eyes twinkling.

Carter's sneakers skidded to a stop. "Dad! How did you know?" Her eyes squinted suspiciously. "Do you have my cell phone bugged?" It wasn't as crazy as it sounded. Although her father ran a full-service tackle shop, he had a secret, side job: he was an undercover agent for the Princess Protection Program, a covert organization dedicated to keeping the princesses of the world safe. He had access to all sorts of spy gear.

Her father laughed. "Tempting, but no. Rosie called me first to make sure it was okay."

Carter nodded. Her best friend was very big on protocol. Of course she would have asked Mr. Mason's permission before spilling the beans to Carter.

"Wait a minute," Carter said, thinking. "You wanted me to help out at the Bait Shack over spring break. Now, suddenly, you're okay with me heading off on vacation with Rosie?"

Her father gave her a smile. "Well, I wouldn't exactly call it a vacation. It's a pretty impressive conference, Carter. The Princess Summit is about making connections—helping attendees learn what it means to be a modern royal and showing them they aren't alone in their experience by creating bonds of friendship and reliance. It's a great opportunity for Rosie—and also for you."

Carter frowned. "Yeah, but Rosie said it wasn't *all* work. She told me that the hotel where the summit's held is superfancy, and that there would be lots of fun things to do. Getting-to-know-you activities, swimming, cool workshops. Stuff like that." Rosie had also mentioned that there would be boys there, too, but Carter decided to keep that to herself.

"That's right," Mr. Mason agreed. "And somewhere in all those activities, I'm sure you'll learn something that you can apply as service credit on your transcript at Lake Monroe High."

Carter rolled her eyes. That's Dad—always thinking.

"Did Rosie tell you that I have to say I'm her assistant?" Carter asked. That had been the one part of the plan she wasn't too crazy about. Not that she wouldn't do anything for Rosie. She totally would. It was more that she didn't want to let Rosie down by saying or doing something that would embarrass her royal best friend.

"She did," her father said. "I told her that after all the years you've helped out here at the Bait Shack, assisting your best friend at the Princess Summit would be a piece of cake."

"So . . . I can go?" Carter blurted out,

flipping open her cell phone to quickly text her friend.

Baitgirl: i'm in!

Her dad nodded. "But first?" He squirted the hose at Carter's feet, making her squeal. "Help me carry in these bait buckets, would you?"

Chapter 2

"This is unbelievable," Carter said, gaping as she and Rosie climbed out of the sleek black limousine underneath the hotel's ginormous entrance awning. The week since Rosie had called to invite Carter to attend the Princess Summit had flown by, and now here they were, ready to start their adventure.

"I agree, it is quite beautiful," Rosie said.

"No, I mean, it's unbelievable that I have no idea where I am," Carter said. For security reasons, the summit kept its location private. No media were allowed, giving the royals a much-needed break from the prying eyes and questions of reporters. Carter hadn't even been allowed to bring her cell phone. She had boarded a private jet in Louisiana earlier that morning, and when the plane had landed a few hours later, Rosie was waiting for her in a limo.

Rosie giggled. "I do not know where we are either, Carter," she told her friend. "But I do know it is secluded!" They'd driven for miles along a winding road through beautiful woods to the resort, which was nestled in the foothills of a breathtaking mountain range. Rosie took her by the arm. "Come, Carter. Let's go check in!"

Carter turned to grab her suitcase, but a uniformed bellhop had already placed the girls' belongings on a cart and was pulling it inside the main entrance.

Around them cars carrying other royal guests were pulling up. Carter held her breath as they walked past gigantic planters filled with bright red geraniums toward the hotel's revolving glass doors. "This is the coolest," she said as they entered the massive lobby.

The place was amazing—sky-high windows, gleaming floors, and wall-to-wall VIPS. Everywhere she looked, Carter saw royals chatting, laughing, and hugging one another. Speakers were playing rock music, and the summit staff was passing out cups of fruit punch and water.

Most everyone was wearing regular clothes, though Carter did spot two girls in sparkly tiaras that she had a feeling didn't come from the party store. "I guess it's like a royalty reunion for you," she told Rosie as they walked toward a table with a sign that read SUMMIT CHECK-IN. "Rosie?" But her friend wasn't listening. Instead she was waving happily to someone across the room.

Carter followed Rosie's gaze. A guy

with blond hair and dimples was waving back.

"Who's that?" Carter asked, raising a curious eyebrow. Rosie hadn't mentioned knowing any of the princes who would be there.

"Prince Darius," Rosie whispered out of the side of her mouth. "Our families vacationed in Italy when we were in elementary school. I haven't seen him in a long time, but I recognize his face from his family's annual Christmas card."

"He definitely didn't forget you," Carter told a now-blushing Rosie. "And he gets bonus points for growing up supercute."

"Shhh!" Rosie hushed her. "I'm here for Costa Luna, Carter, not for romance."

"Oh, *right*. Okay," Carter said, sneaking a peek at the prince. He was talking and laughing with a large group of guys. We'll see about that, she thought.

"Welcome to the Prince and Princess Summit," a woman with long brown hair and beautiful brown eyes said to them when they reached the table. She wore a gold name tag that read JULIE. She checked their names off a master list.

"How do you know who we are?" Carter asked.

Julie smiled. "Everyone here is a priority for us. Even assistants such as yourself, Carter. We want to make this a wonderful experience for both you and Queen Rosalinda."

"Wow. I mean, thanks," Carter said, impressed, as the woman passed each of them a thick peach-colored folder with the words PRINCESS SUMMIT embossed in gold foil on the front. "I've had teachers who didn't even know my name until, like, the final semester."

Julie smiled. "The resort is unparalleled for its outstanding amenities and beautiful grounds, with acres of land devoted to sports such as golf and tennis and horseback riding. And with fifty suites and hundreds of individual hotel rooms, it's one of the biggest luxury properties in the country."

"And that country would be . . ." Carter tried.

Julie didn't bite. "I'm certain you'll have a wonderful stay here. Inside your folders, you'll find your individualized schedules for the summit, a map of the grounds, some useful information about the program, and a bar-coded security bracelet we ask that you wear at all times, as it will identify you as a participant in the Princess Summit."

"Are there guests staying at the resort who aren't part of the summit?" Rosie asked.

Julie shook her head. "No. But the bracelets are just an added security measure for us in case someone tries to slip in unawares." She smiled. "With the level of security we have this week, that's highly unlikely. The resort has hosted distinguished guests from around the world, including numerous heads of state. Security is top-notch."

She checked a clipboarded list. "Now, Your Highness and Carter, you will both be staying in suite seventeen seventy-eight, along with three other summit attendees." She handed them each a card key and showed them where the suite was on a huge map of the resort. "Your suitemates have already checked in."

"Who are they?" Carter asked, wondering if it could be any of the royals she had met since becoming Rosie's friend.

"You're rooming with the Princesses Claire, Heidi, and Arianna," Julie said. She smiled up at them over her clipboard. "You'll all be great friends when the summit is over. Enjoy!"

"Thank you," Rosie said, beaming. She linked arms with Carter. "Let's go see if the other princesses are in the suite. Maybe we can all hang out together!"

"Maybe," Carter said, glancing over at a girl wearing a bright pink sundress with matching shoes and sunglasses. She carried a small bright pink bag from which a tiny dog with a matching pink collar was poking its head out. "Are you sure they're going to believe I'm your assistant?"

Rosie nodded. "Trust me, Carter, it will be fine. But, just to be sure . . ." She handed Carter her welcome folder and her heavier-than-it-looked purse. "Better?"

"Bummer. Looks like this room has already been claimed," Carter said when she and Rosie peeked inside the first bedroom. They had taken the elevator up to the bright, airy suite, which contained a formal living room with a couch, chairs, and a coffee table, a huge bathroom, and two bedrooms. On one of the double beds a sweater and a huge leather satchel sat on top of a puffy down comforter, and on the other bed were a stuffed teddy bear and a monogrammed pillow that said ARIANNA in navy script.

"So we'll take the other bedroom," Rosie said easily, walking across the foyer separating the two rooms.

"I bet you anything they left us the smaller one," Carter mumbled as they walked inside. The room was the same size ... with two beds, and a frowning girl sitting on one of them.

"Hello," Rosie said, walking over and extending her hand. "I'm Queen Rosalinda Marie Montoya Fiore of the principality of Costa Luna. My friends call me Rosie."

"Ahhh. Rosalinda. I was wondering if you were going to show up. I'm Claire," the girl said coolly. She wore a leather headband over her short brown hair, and had on a white tank top and gray shorts.

Remember, you're doing this for Rosie, Carter thought as she put on a cheerful smile. "It's nice to meet you, Your Highness. I'm Carter Mason. Queen Rosie's assistant."

The girl gave her an appraising look. "Hmmm. That explains it."

Carter smiled even wider. The sooner she and Rosie could get out of there, the better. But . . . "Um, there's only one bed left," Carter said, looking over at it. "And five of us are supposed to be in the suite, right?"

"Gee, we can't pull the wool over your eyes," the girl said, then gave a little shrug. "One of you stays here. The other gets the twin sleeper in the other room."

Carter's shoulders fell. Not only did they

have to split up, one of them got a pullout bed? So unfair.

"It is the early bird that catches the worm," Rosie said good-naturedly.

Carter grimaced, reminded of her job at the Bait Shack back home. "Please. No worm talk." Resigned to her fate, she began walking out of the room. "Anybody know how to open one of those things?"

Rosie motioned for her to wait. "Carter, I will take the pullout bed. No, no, I insist," she said, holding up her hand as Carter started to protest. "Really, I do not mind."

Carter shot a look at Princess Claire . . . the girl hadn't just rolled her eyes, had she? "Well . . . if you're sure," Carter said quietly to her friend. Rosie was being incredibly generous.

Rosie gave a firm nod. "Absolutely. Although I wish we could room together, it will be good to get to know new people.

Besides," she said, lowering her voice, "you make friends fast, Carter."

"Um . . . okay." Carter took a deep breath. She really didn't want to room with a nervy stranger—especially one who seemed as snooty as Princess Claire—but if Rosie was willing to sleep in a tiny foldout bed, how could she complain?

Just then there was a light rap on the door. The bellhop had arrived with Rosie's and Carter's luggage. "Thanks," Carter said as the man unloaded her things and turned the cart toward the other bedroom, following Rosie's lead.

"Wow, I haven't seen luggage like that before," Claire said, wrinkling her nose as she eyed Carter's camouflage-print duffel and decal-covered suitcase. "It's . . . different."

"I try to pack light," Carter said politely, biting back her annoyance. "*I* wanted to make sure my roommate had plenty of room for *her* stuff." And it was a good thing she had. There was a brown leather trunk, three suitcases, two apparel bags, and a turquoise duffel stacked in the small closet—all belonging to Princess Claire.

"Room assignments aren't given out until check-in for a reason," Claire said nonchalantly. She watched as Carter opened her suitcase and hung up a dress and some tops. "That way no one can complain about their assignment or request another roommate."

Carter nodded, rummaging around for her toothbrush. She knew she shouldn't make snap judgments, but Claire was exactly the kind of person she couldn't stand: snooty and bratty. The kind of princess Carter had at first expected Rosie to be like.

"Carter?" Rosie stuck her head into the room. Her cheeks were flushed with excitement. "I just found out that our first activity starts in fifteen minutes!" she said breathlessly. "It's a welcome tea!"

Carter looked down at her shorts and tank top. "I don't suppose—"

"Definitely not," Rosie said, finishing Carter's sentence. "Now, go get dressed! There's no second chance to make a good first impression."

As Rosie hurried back to her room to change, Carter thought about Princess Claire and her snobby attitude. She didn't want to be the kind of person who judged someone after just one encounter.

I'll give her another chance, Carter decided.

After all, she didn't really have a choice.

"Welcome, welcome." A security officer in a dark blue suit held up a scanner and Rosie obligingly held up her wrist so he could scan her pale purple security bracelet.

"A pleasure to see you, Your Highness." The officer reached into a basket and handed Rosie a gold name tag with ROSALINDA engraved on it. "Enjoy."

Thanking her, Rosie walked under a large archway covered with flowers into a gorgeous outdoor garden. A large tent was set up with tables covered in pink linen tablecloths. Thinly sliced strawberries floated in punch bowls, and urns filled with hot water for tea sat next to carafes of milk.

The tent was filling up quickly with young royals. Rosie walked across the lawn, smiling at familiar faces. On her left, a prince and princess were in a passionate discussion about water conservation; on her right, four princesses were chatting about their summer plans.

Rosie wanted to pinch herself. This was exactly how she had imagined the Prince and Princess Summit—a place where people just like her could hang out, relax, and learn a little something about how to do the best job they could as rulers. Rosie wanted to be the best queen Costa Luna had ever seen, and the summit was going to help her do just that.

"There are so many choices," she said to a young woman standing near a table, pouring herself a cup of hot water and perusing a wooden tea chest filled with a variety of tea bags.

"And this is the easy part. The dessert trays are where things get complicated," the young woman replied with a conspiratorial whisper. She had shoulder-length blond hair and rosy cheeks.

Rosie looked over at a table filled with tiered plates of tea sandwiches, pastries, and scones. Young royals were milling about with dessert plates, sampling the goodies.

"If only all of our decisions could be like this," Rosie said, smiling.

The young woman's gold-plated name tag glinted in a ray of sunlight. HEIDI.

"Princess Heidi of Pengova!" Rosie exclaimed, making the connection. "I am Rosie, your roommate—well, at least one of them. I just arrived from Costa Luna a little while ago."

"Queen Rosalinda!" Heidi said warmly, taking Rosie's hand. "How nice to finally meet you. I've heard such nice things about your country."

"And I, yours." Rosie helped herself to a cup of Earl Grey tea. "But please, call me Rosie." The instructions inside the summit folder had requested that the attendees refrain from addressing each other using royal titles, but it was a hard habit to break.

"Do you like to play golf?" Heidi asked, her face lighting up. "They have a championship golf course here that has hosted many world-class tournaments."

Regretfully, Rosie shook her head. "The only time I played golf was with my fri—I mean, my assistant, Carter. And it was mini golf," Rosie said. "So I do not think that counts."

Heidi smiled. "There are so many activities here. Maybe we can find one we both like and do it together."

"That would be lovely," Rosie said. She'd been at the summit only a few hours and already she felt as if she had made a new friend.

They were just about to head over to the buffet table when a girl's nasal voice interrupted them. "I should have known they'd put us together."

Heidi gasped. "*You* are our third roommate? No!"

"Unfortunately, yes."

Rosie vaguely recognized the newcomer from television news shows and magazines. She was a tall girl with a silky black bob, big blue eyes, and a serious scowl. She was from Manchara, a country that bordered the Mediterranean Sea in the south of Europe.

"Hello, Rosie." The girl gave a curt nod of recognition. "I am Arianna Silano. I hate to spoil the party, but this is a serious problem, and unfortunately it appears that you're going to be stuck in the middle of it."

Heidi put down her teacup. "I'm sure we can get our suite assignment changed," she said, her voice rising. Several people glanced over, curious. She crossed her arms. "It would be impossible for me to live in such a situation."

"Ladies? I'm sorry," a Princess Summit team leader in khaki shorts and a pink polo shirt with matching baseball cap had materialized at their side. "I couldn't help but overhear your conversation. Your suite assignment and the rooms you have chosen stay as is for the duration of the summit. Learning to live together is the first step toward a deeper understanding of our commonalities and differences." She gave them a meaningful glance before heading off into the crowd.

"The only thing I understand is that my family is going to be extremely upset when they find out I have to sleep in the same room as *her*," Heidi said, looking as if she might burst into tears at any moment. "Rosie, if you'll excuse me." She turned on her high heels and hurried out into the sunshine of the garden.

"Our parents despise each other," Arianna confirmed. "Manchara and Pengova have a common border, and it has caused many problems." She sniffed. "Of course, the unreasonable demands of the Zedler family are what have caused so much friction. They are just so difficult to deal with, as evidenced by Princess Heidi's behavior."

"I—I hope that you find common ground during the Princess Summit," Rosie said, trying to sound more certain than she felt. A waiter passed by with a tray of mini quiches and she eagerly took one, happy to have a diversion.

I *had* hoped to practice my diplomatic skills this week, Rosie thought, taking a delicate bite. She just hadn't anticipated putting them to the test on her first day!

Chapter 3

*R*osie's eyes fluttered open. She'd been in the middle of a wonderful dream—sitting on the edge of the dock back at Carter's house in Louisiana, letting her feet dangle over the cool lake water as she sipped a glass of freshly squeezed lemonade.

Then a duck swam over to her and began quacking. And then another. And another.

Quack, quack, quack. "What? Huh?" She sat up, rubbing her eyes. She wasn't on the dock. She wasn't even in her own bed.

She was curled up in the hotel suite's twin sleeper underneath a soft down comforter.

And the quacking? More like the

unrolling and ripping off of masking tape, thanks to Arianna, who was on her knees, tape roll in hand.

"Can you tell me why you are placing tape in the middle of our room at"—she squinted at the clock—"seven twenty-five in the morning?" Rosie asked, stretching in her oversized T-shirt.

Arianna stood up. She was already dressed in a blue top that matched her eyes and an ivory miniskirt with front flap pockets. She wore a look of determination on her pinched face. "We need to establish boundaries. That's the only way we're going to get through this summit without killing each other."

"Killing us, you mean," Heidi snapped. She was sitting up in her bed, her blond hair rumpled. A notebook lay next to her. "Rosalinda has nothing to do with this. Leave her out of it."

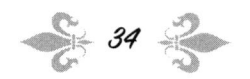

"I know it's difficult for you, but chill, Heidi." Arianna put down her final piece of tape. "There. No confusion."

But Rosie was more confused than ever. The plush green carpet now looked like a crazy grid of tape. "Um . . . what do these lines mean exactly?" she asked, even though she wasn't sure she wanted to hear the answer.

"My space is here," Arianna said, pointing to her bed. "When I need to cross the room I'll use this thoroughfare."

"Thoroughfare?" Rosie repeated, staring at the long, narrow strip of carpet marked off by tape, which Arianna indicated.

"If everyone sticks to the plan, we'll have no issues," Arianna insisted. "Heidi, that's your thoroughfare," she said, pointing to another strip next to her bed. "And Rosie, you're neutral. You can walk wherever you want."

"That's quite generous," Rosie said, taking a deep breath. She knew the situation was fragile. But she hoped that today would be a step in the right direction . . . that is, if everyone stepped where they were supposed to.

Heidi ripped a page from her notebook and leaped off her bed.

"I've taken the liberty of creating a schedule for the bathroom," she said, striding out the bedroom door. "With five of us and one shower, we definitely need organization."

"And I suppose you're first," Arianna called after her, obviously annoyed.

The only response was Heidi slamming the bathroom door shut behind her.

Rosie bit her lip as she met Arianna's gaze. "Call me crazy, but something tells me you are last."

Rosie hadn't thought things could get worse.

But after breakfast, the pranks just kept coming.

While Arianna, Carter, and Rosie had gone downstairs to grab some juice and yogurt, Heidi said she wasn't hungry. She stayed in the suite and when the rest of the girls returned later, Rosie was shocked.

The princess had taken it upon herself to push all of Arianna's clothes to the side of their shared closet . . . and to take most of the space for herself.

"You moved my clothes?" Arianna said when she saw what Heidi had done.

Carter stayed in the foyer as Rosie listened to her roommates bicker. She's smart not to get too close, Rosie thought, as Arianna and Heidi confronted each other.

"It had to be done," Heidi said, giving a helpless shrug. "My clothes are made of the most delicate fabrics. I have dresses by the most famous designers in Europe—they must *breathe*. They can't be shoved next to—to sweatshirts!"

Arianna looked like she was ready to explode. "That's a vintage cashmere sweater my mother special ordered for me!" she exclaimed, taking it out of the closet to smooth an imaginary wrinkle.

Rosie hurriedly stepped between them. "Let's make things simple, shall we?" She pulled off the long ribbon that was holding her hair back from her face and tied it in the middle of the closet rod. "On the left, Arianna. On the right, Heidi. I didn't unpack yet, and if I do need to hang something up I will divide my clothes equally."

Rosie looked over at the desk clock. The first meeting of the summit was about to begin, and everyone was expected to attend. "Now, we have to be at our first meeting in ten minutes," she said calmly. "Would you two like to accompany me and Ca—I mean, my assistant downstairs?"

"I'm not leaving until she does," Arianna said, her arms folded tightly over her chest.

"Well, I'm not leaving until *you* do," Heidi shot back.

"So, if we all go down together..." Rosie ventured cautiously.

But neither princess heard her. They were too busy arguing over the floor space in the closet where their shoes would go.

Rosie and Carter walked out of the suite.

"Can you believe them?" Carter asked, incredulous.

Rosie gave a disheartened shrug. "I thought people would be excited to be here. Instead, they're fighting over silly things like closet space and bathroom schedules."

"Maybe that's the point," Carter said, pushing the elevator button. "It's the dumb things that spin into the worst headaches."

"All this arguing is giving *me* a headache," Rosie said. "And this roommate situation is a prescription I don't need . . . a prescription for disaster."

When she had registered for the summit, Carter had been given a list of interest areas to choose from: health care, literacy, a world in crisis, living green, arts and culture, and wealth and poverty.

Carter picked living green.

"I knew you'd pick arts and culture," she said to Rosie as they stood in front of a flat-screen TV in the hotel lobby which indicated where the various groups were meeting. "You've already done so much for Costa Luna . . . opening a gallery for young artists to showcase their work. You could practically teach this session! It's so you."

"It is easy when you are passionate about something," Rosie said modestly. "It was hard to choose, though," she admitted. "I kept changing my mind. There is so much to learn, I want to do it all!"

"Can you imagine if I'd picked literacy?" Carter said, rolling her eyes. "I'd be stuck listening to Claire ramble on about *ah-mazing* books and *dahling* libraries." When her roommate had announced her choice, Carter had resisted the urge to fist-bump her with joy that they weren't going to be together. While Claire wasn't doing anything nearly as ridiculous as Heidi and Arianna, Carter's patience was being tested. Claire spent most of her time in their room gossiping with her friends back home about the people she'd just met. And the floor was littered with her dirty clothes. Carter was happy to have a break from her roommate, even if it was only for a couple of hours. "That is, assuming Claire *is* literate."

"Carter!" Then Rosie giggled. "I have to

confess that it is kind of funny that Heidi and Arianna both chose 'a world in crisis.'"

"I guess they wanted to stick with what they know best," Carter said.

"I feel sorry for their leader!" Then Rosie's tone turned serious. "But perhaps it will help them. Something needs to change for those girls."

Carter and Rosie made plans to meet up for lunch and then went off to their groups.

As she walked into a meeting room filled with tables of chatting royals and enough security guards for a rock concert, Carter spotted a familiar face: Prince Darius. He smiled at her kindly. Carter scanned her bracelet and then walked over to take the chair beside him.

"You are here at the summit with Rosalinda, yes?" the prince asked after introducing himself.

"Yes. I'm her assistant, Carter," she said,

shaking his hand. "Queens get, um, to bring someone with them. Like . . . like a buddy system." She would have liked to have told him the truth about who she was, but she didn't dare.

"We used to go on vacation together. We were very young. I am happy to see her again," the prince told Carter, his face brightening. "I'm looking forward to catching up."

Before Carter could respond, the group's facilitator came in and began the session. The idea was that each group would work together throughout the summit to generate new ideas.

Carter thought about a flytying class she'd taken last summer. Wet flies, nymphs, streamers . . . she'd shared the cool new tying techniques with the customers at the Bait Shack. This was the same in theory . . . but with huge rewards. The royals could share what they learned with their *entire countries!*

This is such a cool opportunity, Carter thought as she listened to all the different ideas. And soon she was raising her hand to give her opinion.

"Carpooling is pretty big where I live," Carter said. "Maybe you guys could, um, share limos sometimes? Or fly economy—those private jets have really bad carbon footprints, you know."

A few of the royals shrugged, and a lot of them wore blank stares. "Maybe," one princess said, but she didn't sound too excited.

"And at my school, we bring reusable aluminum water bottles instead of plastic ones," Carter continued. "And we recycle batteries and cell phones and stuff."

One prince tapped his chin. "Hmmm. We couldn't do that with our own phones for security reasons, but maybe we could implement it for our subjects?"

"You can get the data erased," Prince Darius spoke up. "I've done it, and so far there have been no problems. I'm involved with a program that collects cell phones, sells them to a company that recycles them, and gives the money to three specific charities."

As the group began to talk excitedly about starting similar programs where they each lived, Carter snuck a peek at Prince Darius. He was scribbling notes and animatedly participating in the dialogue. Not only was he cute and seemed interested in Rosie, he was a good-deed doer back in his country.

In short, Prince Darius was perfect boyfriend material for a queen.

Okay, okay, Carter knew that Rosie wasn't looking for a boyfriend—she was too busy for a serious relationship. But a little fun and flirting with a family friend who happened to be a prince?

Carter rocked back in her seat, smiling to herself. Who better than her to play matchmaker to two sweet, unsuspecting royals?

Nobody, that's who.

Chapter 4

"I'm not sure this is such a good idea," Heidi said, warily looking up at the huge outdoor rock-climbing tower. The tower sat adjacent to a large playground at the eastern corner of the main grounds. Heidi and Rosie were among a group of eight royals who had chosen climbing as their morning team-building activity.

Rosie fought back a yawn. She'd had an incredibly interesting but tiring day yesterday attending her arts and culture session in the morning, a seminar on treaties in the afternoon, and then, after dinner, doing one of her favorite activities with Carter:

bowling! She'd been looking forward to a good night's rest, but that had been wishful thinking. Arianna and Heidi just couldn't stop fighting long enough for Rosie to fall asleep.

The head instructor, a dark-haired guy named Joe, stepped forward. "We wouldn't let anything happen to you," he assured the group. "Your safety is our primary concern."

Rosie nodded, trying to calm her own nerves. The tower was almost fifty feet tall, and even though they were in a group designated for beginners, it was still pretty intimidating. She snuck a glance toward the playground, which looked a lot more appealing.

Then, she steadied her shoulders and reached over to squeeze Heidi's hand. "We can do this. Piece of cake." Rosie and Carter had come up with a plan over breakfast: by splitting up Arianna and Heidi, they might be able to discover the *real* cause of the age-old feud—and maybe even come up with a solution.

But maybe we should have found an activity that didn't involve body harnesses, Rosie thought as Joe showed the group how to put on the necessary gear.

"This isn't very comfortable," Heidi said, wiggling her toes in her rubber climbing shoes.

Joe chuckled. "We're not big on comfort, but we are big on safety." He checked to make sure that everyone's harness fit snugly so no one would slip out during their climb.

Next he showed them the gear they would need, including ropes and belay devices. "Before you can climb, you need to learn how to belay."

Rosie learned that the belayer was the person who kept you safe and helped make sure you got back to the ground in one piece.

After going over how to tie a knot and getting answers to a few questions, the group was ready to climb.

The royals lined up to take their turns at the wall. They would work in pairs: one person would be the climber and one person would be the belayer, holding the rope to make sure the person climbing didn't fall. Rosie was going to climb first, while Heidi supported her from the ground.

"Use the step-through technique," Heidi said as Rosie looked up at the wall looming large in front of her.

"Okay," she said, remembering what they had gone over with Joe. Her left foot was on the hold—a hard plastic piece jutting out from the wall—and her hands were gripping holds above each of her shoulders. Taking a deep breath, Rosie moved her right leg above her left, directly under her hands, and found the hold.

"That's it!" Heidi called from below. "Remember, climb with your legs."

With Heidi encouraging her, Rosie focused on taking one step at a time. Before she knew it, she was at the top.

"Yay, you!" Heidi called from below, and Rosie felt a rush of pride. She'd done it!

Joe had talked about all the benefits of climbing—building self-confidence, learning to work together as a team—and after successfully completing her first climb and then helping Heidi do the same thing, Rosie saw how true Joe's words were.

"That was tremendous," Heidi said as they began taking off their gear. Her rosy cheeks were even rosier. "A couple of people were talking about coming again tomorrow, and I think I might join them. Would you want to do it again?"

Rosie shrugged. "Maybe." She turned to Heidi. "I wish we'd had more of a chance to talk. You know, get to know each other."

"You probably think I'm a terrible person after all the things Arianna has been saying about me," Heidi admitted.

Rosie shook her head. "Of course not. Every story has two sides. What is yours, Heidi?"

Heidi exhaled slowly. "The Silano family is notorious for their bad behavior. They allow cafés and hotels to be built right on the border between our countries and attempt to claim a little more land every year."

"So the feud is over where exactly the border is?" Rosie asked, trying to clarify the situation for herself.

"Yes, but it's also much more personal. The Silanos use every opportunity to slander us in the newspapers and news journals. You should hear the stories my grandfather tells." Then Heidi shook her head. "On second thought, I would not want you to hear them. They are too vile."

Rosie handed her harness to Joe. *I wonder how things are going for Carter?* she thought. Rosie felt like she had definitely solidified her friendship with Heidi. But as for making headway toward solving the feud . . . not so much.

"So are you having fun here?" Carter asked as she and Arianna sat side by side in the spa's nail salon. She'd overheard Arianna booking an appointment for a pedicure, and had immediately booked an appointment for herself, too. And amazingly, they'd ended up sitting next to one another in white leather chairs. Bubbling soaking tubs sat at their feet while soothing music played and vanilla-scented candles burned.

It was the perfect opportunity to relax . . . and get to the bottom of things.

Arianna shrugged, not looking up from the magazine she was reading. "Other than my horrendous roommate situation, it's okay. Though I'm not crazy about all the outdoor activities they keep pushing on us. They assume that just because we're royals we must love to ride horses. I'll take my customized scooter any day, thank you very much."

The nail technician buffed Carter's nails, then motioned for her to soak her feet in the warm, fizzy bath.

Carter sighed blissfully. The water felt so good! "But . . . what are you and Heidi even mad about, anyway? Do you even know?"

"They just can't respect our border. We've made it clear where their land ends and ours begins, but for some reason, they always find a way to 'accidentally' use our land and expect us to just go along with it." A different nail technician began slathering

Arianna's calves with a peppermint body scrub.

"I don't blame you for being upset," Carter said diplomatically.

"And the Zedlers have a history of trashing my family in the press," Arianna continued, scowling. "You should hear the stories my grandmother tells. They're horrible!"

"Hmmm." Carter tried to remember if she had heard anything about Arianna's family. It would make her pretty angry if someone was saying mean stuff about her and her dad. "But maybe now's the time to stop fighting," Carter tried with a hopeful expression. "Maybe—"

"Maybe you don't know what you're talking about," Arianna blurted out as the technician began to massage her feet. "Carter, I know you're just trying to help, but you don't really understand the situation. One hundred years of fighting isn't something we can just put behind us like a bad day, you know?"

"But don't you think—"

Arianna groaned. "Carter—I came here for a pedicure, not the third degree. Can we not talk about it anymore? Please?"

Carter flushed. "No. Sure. I'm sorry." She leaned back in her chair and closed her eyes. She was going to need a massage just to get over the stress of this pedicure!

"Okay, let me get this straight. Heidi told you that the Silanos are trying to take their land," Carter said, taking a handful of popcorn from the bucket she was sharing with Rosie. They were in the hotel's 300-seat private movie theater, waiting for *Sandcastle Summer* to start. Carter found it incredible that a movie most people wouldn't get to see for another two weeks was having a special screening here at the summit. Royal life could be pretty cool.

Rosie nodded. "That is correct."

"And Heidi's grandfather has some terrible stories about what the Silano family has done."

Rosie nodded again. "That is correct."

Carter snorted. "That is crazy, Rosie, because that's exactly what Arianna told me about the Zedlers! Except her *grandmother* is the one who has terrible stories about the Silanos!"

"Clearly each girl feels that she is telling the truth," Rosie said thoughtfully. She took a dainty sip of soda.

"And they hate each other, Rosie."

Rosie shook her head. "I don't think they do, Carter. I think they are only following the example of their families."

Suddenly the lights dimmed. The movie was about to start.

A group of boys came loping down the center aisle of the theater and stepped into their row.

"Are these seats taken?" the first boy asked Rosie.

"Oh, no. Please," Rosie whispered.

Carter leaned forward in her seat, recognizing the boy's voice. Yes! It was Prince Darius—with a couple of his friends: Prince Gordon and Prince Eduard.

"I thought that was you, Rosie," Darius whispered, and Carter could see his gleaming smile in the dark.

"It is me," Rosie replied, and Carter didn't have to see her face to know that her best friend was turning three shades of red right now.

The matchmaking gods were definitely smiling on them.

Rosie knew that the movie had something

to do with sandcastles and summer, but that was about all she knew. She couldn't pay attention to the story or the characters or the plot. She couldn't even say who the actors were in the film. Or if it was a comedy or a drama.

All she could do was think about who was sitting next to her. A supercute boy who happened to be her childhood friend Darius, all grown up.

Rosie would never tell Carter this—or, at least not until they were home—but . . . she really did like Prince Darius. He was kind, funny, and warm—and each time she saw him, he seemed to smile at her even more. She was nervous, though, and when she was nervous, she resorted to the one thing that got her through the most difficult situations: she remained polite and formal.

Because . . . because what if they went out on a date? What would her subjects say?

If anything even remotely romantic were to happen, would it mean that Costa Luna agreed with Darius's country's policies?

I don't even know what his country's policies are! she thought. Rosie's knee brushed Darius's, and she jumped as if electrocuted.

She kept her hands clasped primly in her lap and her eyes fixed firmly on the movie screen. Because if she couldn't even keep her mind focused on a movie, who knew the kind of national-security details she might let slip if Darius tried to hold her hand?

Dating was complicated enough as it was. Dating royalty—when you *were* royalty? Complicated didn't even come close.

Chapter 5

The next morning, Rosie was up and dressed before any of the other girls in the suite. After neatly crossing her name off the bathroom schedule with a black pen (she was third on the list), Rosie tiptoed into Carter's room. Carter was still asleep, her pillow over her head.

Rosie left a handwritten note under Carter's pillow explaining where she would be and tiptoed back out. All the royals had leadership workshops that morning; Carter would be able to sleep in.

I hope she does something fun, Rosie thought. She nodded at the security officers as she stepped into the elevator and headed down to the lobby. For once, Arianna and Heidi had been too tired to argue much last night, but Rosie had still tossed and turned in her pullout bed.

She hadn't been able to stop thinking about Prince Darius.

When they had said good-bye after the movie, Rosie had a weird feeling that the prince had wanted to talk with her some more. But he hadn't. Maybe he was too shy to approach her when she was with her friend. Or maybe he felt funny in front of *his* friends.

Or maybe I'm just imagining the whole thing, Rosie thought, stopping by the lobby snack cart to pick up a bottle of apple juice and a cranberry muffin. The muffin reminded her of the delicious baked goods the chef was always whipping up in the kitchen back home, and suddenly her mind flitted to Costa Luna.

Rosie wondered how everyone was—her mother, Sophia; Mr. Elegante, the royal dress designer; and her many staff members, who were more like friends than employees. Rosie understood why the Princess Summit didn't want attendees to have cell phones—it was very tempting to call home every day or spend time texting.

But then Rosie brightened. She thought about all she was learning and how much her country and her people would benefit. For now, she would put her thoughts of the prince aside.

The seminar had been great—and now it was free time for the afternoon. Rosie, Carter, and a couple of the other princesses—Margret and Stephanie—were just finishing their lunch on the hotel's poolside terrace when Rosie felt a gentle tap on her shoulder. She looked up to see blond hair, warm brown eyes, dimples . . . Prince Darius!

He smiled down at her, looking cute in his gray-and-baby-blue–striped polo and stone-colored cargo shorts. "Hello, Rosalinda. I was wondering if you would like to go horseback riding with me this afternoon. The concierge told me there are some beautiful trails here and a stable of first-class horses."

Rosie swallowed her iced tea, hesitating. She had been discussing how a prominent salsa band from her country might be able to perform in Margret's country while a classical dance troop from Margret's homeland could visit Costa Luna.

"We can definitely talk about the music stuff later," Margret chimed in, a coy smile on her face. Rosie had only just met her, but she could tell the princess loved to gossip about the princes and princesses at the summit. "I—I made a hair appointment anyway." She fluffed her perfect red curls. "Totally out of control."

Carter and Stephanie, a friendly princess from South America, were nodding animatedly. "And we're joining her," they said in unison.

Rosie looked curiously at Carter. Since when had her friend cared how her hair looked? Normally, Carter pulled her long dark hair back into a ponytail, or shoved it up under a baseball cap. "Oof," Rosie said.

Carter had just given her a not-so-subtle kick under the table.

Rosie turned and smiled up at Darius. Riding with the prince would be a good chance for her to get to know him. She could learn more about Darius's country and his political views. And maybe even find out what kind of music he liked, or what he did for fun back home. She could always meet up with Margret later. "That—that would be fun," she finally said. "But I must tell you—I haven't ridden a horse in quite some time."

"It's like riding a bike," he said. "Once you learn, you never forget." He tilted his head toward the main building. "I'm just going to change . . . meet you in the lobby in twenty minutes?"

"That sounds good," Rosie said as he walked away. The girls leaned in and started talking.

"He *so* likes you!" Margret whispered excitedly.

"He seems so nice," Stephanie said, her eyes wide.

Carter squeezed Rosie's hand. "I'm glad you said yes. I mean, really Rosie, the cultural-appreciation stuff is great and all, but it can definitely wait."

"I just hope I don't say anything . . . stupid," Rosie told them, feeling excited and anxious all at once.

Carter shook her head. "Rosie, in all the time I've known you, you always manage to come off completely cool and elegant. Even when you were covered head to toe in frozen yogurt! You're not like me—queen of the crazy guy mishaps. Once I sat talking to this guy I liked after lunch, and later, when I looked in my locker mirror, I realized I had a piece of lettuce stuck between my front teeth. It was so embarrassing."

The other princesses cringed, sympathetically.

"That would be bad, yes," Rosie commiserated. "But for a princess, one careless remark could set off an entire international incident!"

Carter hopped up from her chair and pushed it under the table. "That's not going to happen to you, trust me. You're not a lettuce-in-your-teeth kind of girl." She linked arms with Rosie. "Come on, let's go pick out what you're going to wear."

"I thought you had a hair appointment," Rosie teased.

"I'm your assistant, remember?" Carter gave her long brown hair a shake. "My hair can wait. You, looking amazing? Top priority."

Rosie didn't have any riding clothes in her luggage, but she and Carter decided that a pair of straight-leg dark denim jeans and a pretty short-sleeved pink blouse would be just fine. Claire happened to be in the suite when Rosie was getting ready. To Carter's amazement, she pulled out a gorgeous pair of cowboy boots that she offered to let Rosie borrow.

"They're from last year," she said, handing them over. "And they pinch my feet."

"Well, they appear to fit me perfectly,"

Rosie said, admiring the dark brown leather. "Thank you very much. I will take good care of them."

She took off all her jewelry except the security bracelet, and pulled her hair back in a low ponytail. When she got back to the lobby, Darius was waiting for her, and together, they headed down to the equestrian center.

"It is so beautiful here," Rosie said, looking out at the mountains. The sky was a crisp blue, not a cloud for miles, and the air felt cool and fresh, the smell of pine trees lingering on the breeze.

"Yes, there's really no place like it in my country," Darius said as they walked. "We're lucky the summit is held in such a great place. Can you imagine if we were in a desert? Or if they tried to test our endurance and critical thinking by holding it on some frozen tundra?"

"We are at the Prince and Princess Summit, not on a reality show," Rosie said, giggling. "Though it could be kind of funny to see how everyone would react under that kind of pressure!"

The equestrian center offered a variety of programs: carriage rides on the extensive hotel grounds, guided tours on horseback, and private lessons for beginners. Or you could just ride the trails on your own.

That's what Rosie and Darius decided to do. It turned out that Darius was an expert rider. Not only did he horseback ride for fun, he was also an experienced polo player.

They put on riding helmets and went out with a trainer to meet their horses. "Rosie, you'll be riding Sugar," the trainer said as a groom walked a dark brown horse over. "She's very gentle and one of our nicest fillies."

"She is beautiful," Rosie said as Sugar

stood in front of her, saddled and ready for their ride.

Darius would be riding a light caramel-colored horse named Maverick, who the trainer said was excellent for a more experienced rider.

After they had each mounted their horses, the trainer explained the trail markers.

"Nice horsie," Rosie whispered, gathering the reins and squeezing her legs against Sugar. And they were off.

At first Rosie was tense, but the trainer was right—Sugar seemed like the gentlest, most peaceful horse ever. She relaxed, letting Sugar lead the way as she sat back in the saddle.

"So how different is this from riding a polo pony?" Rosie asked, enjoying the feel of the sun on her face and the slight breeze in the air.

Darius laughed. "Probably as different as you would feel riding in one of your horse-drawn carriages. Close your eyes," he told Rosie.

"Are you sure that's a good idea?" she asked as Sugar trotted along.

"These horses have walked these trails a hundred times. Just for a second—I promise."

Rosie did.

"I'm going to try and explain what polo is like. Now, imagine you're on your horse, and the ball is like a blur flying through the air straight at you."

"The horse doesn't get scared?"

"Hopefully not. You need to stay at a gallop, get the ball, and pass it to your teammate or ride downfield and try to make a goal."

Rosie opened her eyes. "I think Sugar is more my speed." Her senses felt even more alive after closing her eyes for a minute.

Sunlight filtered through the trees, and she thought she heard the sound of a tiny brook gurgling in the distance.

"All this land belongs to the hotel?" she asked.

Darius nodded. "Over six thousand acres. I looked through the guidebook we got in our welcome packets, hoping I'd have some time to get out here and ride. The trails run for miles and miles."

"That sounds like the entire size of Costa Luna!" Rosie said, only half exaggerating.

"I was in Costa Luna once, many years ago," Darius said. "I believe my father had a meeting there, and I distinctly remember playing on a swing set in the palace's backyard."

Rosie smiled. "We still have that swing set. When I look at it, it reminds me to stay lighthearted."

"And I also remember you chasing me

around the courtyard trying to get me to kiss you."

Rosie gasped. "Oh, my goodness. Surely that did not happen. I do not remember that!"

Darius wore a slightly devilish expression. "Or maybe that was just wishful thinking."

Rosie felt her cheeks grow warm. She cleared her throat. "There's a lot more to horseback riding than people think," she said, changing the subject. "I'm trying to remember everything—keeping my legs underneath me, my heels down, my arms relaxed."

"Luckily, horses are supersmart. They're primed to react to danger—and they have better vision than we do."

"Good Sugar. Sweet Sugar," Rosie said, hoping her soft voice would make her horse feel calm and reassured.

The horses made their way down a slight

incline and around a bend, where a beautiful lake shimmered in the light. No one was there—no boaters, no swimmers, not even any ducks—and the surface of the water was as smooth as glass.

"It's easy to forget all your problems in a place like this, isn't it?" Darius said, his voice pensive.

"Yes," Rosie said. "Do you feel a lot of pressure back at home in Ileos?"

Darius sighed. "It's strange. I mean, I know how lucky I am. I'm seventeen, finishing up my last year of school before university, and every door I could want to step through is open to me. But . . ."

"But?" Rosie prompted.

Darius shot her an embarrassed look. "I feel kind of ridiculous complaining to you. You've got more pressure on your shoulders than any other teenager I know."

"Costa Luna is not without problems,

but after some recent troubles, things are looking up. We are in a good place."

Darius nodded. "I am very interested in international relations, and my father has given me a lot of responsibility. He feels it will serve me well one day, when I am king."

"Yes. It will," Rosie said, speaking from experience. Suddenly she had a thought. "Do you know anything about the feud between Arianna's and Heidi's families? Your country is close to theirs, right?"

"Unfortunately, yes," Darius said.

"After hearing their stories, Carter and I thought that maybe they could put their differences aside this week and take some steps toward friendship, but I can't even figure out what their differences are. I wonder if they can themselves."

Darius gave Maverick a bit more rein. "It's pretty complicated. The leaders of Manchara and Pengova have been fighting for so long that they aren't paying attention to a real problem that their argument is causing surrounding countries—such as my own."

"Oh, no," Rosie said, biting her lip. "Carter and I think the girls are fighting because they 'have to.' It doesn't seem that they know the root of the feud between the countries—or the damage it is causing."

"It would take much too long to explain, and I believe we have more interesting things to discuss—like perhaps my getting your phone number."

Rosie laughed. "It's possible that can be arranged."

"Soon things are going to have to change for Arianna and Heidi, though." His eyes turned sober. "You met Princess Margret, right? Well, she gets word of things practically before they happen, and I overheard her in the lobby saying that there's been talk about other countries taking action against Manchara and Pengova."

"Maybe that's just idle gossip," Rosie suggested.

Darius shook his head. "No. She's right. Only a small inner circle within my country had discussed a potential plan, so if Margret has heard about it, that means things have developed since I left," he said grimly.

"How did she find out?" Rosie asked.

"Don't know. But it doesn't matter. What does matter is that those two countries come to their senses and end all the fighting." Darius turned to Rosie, and his normally upbeat expression was now one of grim resignation. "Not just for themselves. But for all of us," he said.

Chapter 6

"He was very serious, Carter," Rosie said, biting her lip. The moment she returned from her horseback ride, she had made a beeline to find her friend. Luckily, Carter had been walking through the hotel lobby. Now they were sitting on a flower-patterned couch under a potted palm tree trying to figure out what to do. "Darius said that he overheard Margret saying there's been talk about going into the two countries."

"Like an invasion?" Carter asked, her eyes widening. She looked around the bustling lobby, then lowered her voice. "No offense, but two girls arguing about closet space doesn't sound like an international incident to me."

"It is not about closet space," Rosie said quietly. "The true root of their problems lies much deeper. Remember what Arianna told you at the nail salon? How you can't just get over a century of fighting?"

Carter sighed. "You're right, Rosie. But do they even get it? Do they understand how seriously strained relations are between Manchara and Pengova and that the situation is affecting their neighboring countries?"

"What is that expression, Carter? 'You can't see the forest for the trees?' Arianna and Heidi are focusing so hard on their squabbles that they're missing the fact that their countries are in serious political trouble."

Carter hugged her knees. "We've got to call my dad, Rosie. This is too big for us to handle. We don't want things to get out of hand."

Rosie nodded. "There's a conference room on the second floor that is set up for video chats. I will tell the summit staff to make sure we have a secure connection."

Because if they didn't call Major Mason, they could have a real emergency on their hands.

"So that's it, Dad," Carter said to her father, his face bright and clear on the large TV screen. She and Rosie had just finished telling him what was going on at the summit between the feuding princesses. "We just thought you should know."

"You did the right thing by calling, girls," Mr. Mason said. "But I can assure you both that Arianna and Heidi are safe at the summit. Security is very tight."

"That is true, Major Mason," Rosie confirmed. "There are guards everywhere. Even on the horse trails!"

"And there are also a number of plainclothes officers," Mr. Mason told them. "So in addition to the security presence you see, there's an additional layer of protection throughout the hotel. And the P.P.P. has been and will continue to monitor the situation concerning Arianna and Heidi's homelands."

Carter leaned forward. "Is there anything we should be doing, Dad?"

Her dad's eyes twinkled back at her through the screen. "Just have fun. And don't forget that service credit for school."

"Thanks for reminding me." Carter picked up the videoconference remote and with a wave good-bye, clicked off the screen. Then she turned to Rosie. "You heard what my father said."

"School?" Rosie raised an eyebrow.

"Fun," Carter stood up and pointed out a window to a couple of princesses in bikinis and cover-ups walking out the door. "We've got a few hours before the mixer tonight. Let's hang out at the pool. You never know who will *dare* to be there," she said, giving Rosie a teasing look. "Get it? Dar-i-us?"

"Shhh!" Rosie swatted her with a newspaper. "I am going to have to dunk you for that."

A few hours later, Rosie and Carter stood on one of the many stairways that surrounded the huge outdoor pool. It looked beautiful during the day, but it was absolutely magical at night. Glowing torches framed the perimeter, and candles and flowers floated in the water. Around the pool, tables had been set up so people could talk and sample some of the delicious food from the buffet table. A DJ was blasting music and a large area had been cleared for dancing.

"This is so great," Carter said, shaking

her hips to the beat. She wore a navy dress with spaghetti straps and flat silver sandals that were perfect for dancing.

"It is nice to see everyone having fun," Rosie said, her eyes skimming the crowd.

"Don't speak too soon," Carter said, lifting her chin toward the opposite end of the pool. Arianna and Heidi were facing each other, having some sort of heated argument. Arianna's face was bright red, and Heidi's hands were on her hips.

Rosie sighed. "Maybe I should go talk to them."

"Or maybe you should dance with me."

Rosie turned to see Princes Darius, Gordon, and Eduard behind her.

"I promise I won't embarrass you," Darius said with a smile. He wore khakis and a white oxford shirt with the sleeves rolled up. His shampoo-scented blond hair was still wet from the shower.

"I'm sure you would not embarrass me," Rosie said, hesitating.

"She'd love to," Carter said, giving her friend a tiny push forward. Carter turned to the other princes. "I heard the buffet is to die for, guys. Want to check it out?" And before Rosie could stop her, Carter walked off with two cute princes trailing behind her like puppies.

"Yes. I'd love to," Rosie said to Darius, making a mental note to shake Carter later . . . and then hug her.

Prince Darius took Rosie's hand, and together they made their way toward the middle of the dance floor. All around them princesses and princes were cutting loose, waving their hands in the air and rocking out. Rosie spotted several of her arts-and-culture instructors dancing together.

"You look beautiful," the prince said, smiling at her.

"Thanks," Rosie said, hoping she wasn't blushing too badly. Her long dark hair was pulled back in a casual, slightly messy bun, and she wore a rose-colored chiffon dress and ballet flats.

The DJ was playing one of Rosie's favorite songs. "You lied," Rosie accused good-naturedly as Darius swayed to the beat. "You *are* a good dancer."

"Not really," he shouted over the thumping bass. "I just steal moves from videos."

Rosie giggled. "That could be a disaster, you know."

Darius took her hand and spun her in a circle. "I'm willing to risk it if you are."

They danced to a few more songs. Then the DJ slowed things down, putting on a soft, romantic song.

The prince looked at Rosie. "May I?"

"Sure," Rosie said, feeling her heart race. She'd been having fun being herself, but now she felt nervous all over again.

Darius put one hand on Rosie's hip and held her other hand against his shoulder. They began swaying to the music.

"I don't know about you, but I for one am glad that they included princes at this year's summit," Darius said.

"Oh, I am, too," Rosie told him earnestly. "The princes in my seminars shared some wonderful ideas. They were really inspiring!"

"Mmmm, that's great," the prince said. "But I was thinking more about how nice it is that I got to see you again and spend time with you."

"Oh," Rosie said, unable to hide a smile. "Me, too. Of course, that is what I meant as well." Argh! Being a queen didn't make talking to boys any easier.

It makes it harder, Rosie thought, fretting as they moved back and forth. She took a look around and tried to relax. This was a safe place. No newspaper reporters, no paparazzi . . . just royal teenagers like her having fun.

Or, at least most of them were.

"You don't know what you're talking about!" Arianna yelled. She and Heidi were to one side of the dance floor, pointing fingers at each other.

"No, you're the one who keeps getting in *my* face," Heidi snapped back.

"Me, getting in *your* face?" Arianna jeered. "Well I feel sorry for the poor people of Pengova. They have to look at your family's ugly faces on their money every day!"

The DJ put on a new song—with a thumping baseline. "Let's get this party started, folks!" he shouted, trying to defuse the situation.

But things were taking a decidedly heated turn.

"They've taken this to such a public forum . . . maybe we can help," Rosie said to Darius. He nodded and they made their way through the dancers. A small circle had formed around the fighting princesses.

"Here we go again," someone muttered.

"This is getting kind of old," someone else said.

Princess Margret met Rosie's gaze as they walked over. Margret shook her head. "They just don't get it," she said, her voice carrying in the breeze. "They're fighting over who bumped into who on the dance floor when they should be trying to save what's left of their countries before the military comes in to do it for them."

"What did you say?" Arianna whipped her head toward Margret. "Why are you talking about the military?"

"Yes... what are you blathering about?" Heidi asked, for once seemingly on the same side as her archenemy.

Margret stood there clutching a glass of club soda and a plate of pretzels. "Oh. Well..." She hesitated, obviously more comfortable commenting on the princesses' situation from afar rather than to their faces. "Haven't you watched the news or read a newspaper since you've been here?"

Arianna glared at her. "No."

Heidi drew her eyebrows together in a frown. "Why?"

A few other royals stepped up beside Margret.

One prince spoke out. "You two should stop fighting about stupid stuff and focus on your countries. They're in serious trouble."

All around them people were nodding. "Outside forces are days away from occupying both your homelands," Margret told them.

Arianna and Heidi met each other's gaze, shocked expressions on their faces. Rosie knew what they were thinking—could it really be true?

Without another word, Arianna turned and fled. Heidi, looking pale and shaky, slunk off toward a table in the corner.

"Darius, thank you for the dance," Rosie said, putting her hand lightly on his chest. "But I must—"

"Go," the prince told her, his brown eyes concerned. "We'll talk later. She needs you."

With a grateful smile, Rosie walked over to the table where Heidi sat slumped over, her head in her hands.

"Is it true?" Heidi asked, gazing up at Rosie. "Is Pengova really on the brink of a military occupation?"

Rosie pat her shoulder as she sat down.

"From what I have heard, the threat seems real, Heidi."

A tear slid down Heidi's cheek. "I know Arianna and I have behaved badly here, but I didn't really think that things were that bad between our countries."

Rosie gave what she hoped was a comforting smile. "You could not be in a better place. That is why you're here, isn't it? To work on getting to know other royals and build friendships."

"Friendship?" Heidi reached into her evening bag to take out a tissue. "We're about as far from being friends as a cat and mouse."

"The summit isn't over yet," Rosie gently reminded her. "Maybe you can use the remaining time here to work on healing the feud between your families."

Heidi blew her nose, then shrugged. "I guess it wouldn't hurt," she said in a soft voice.

Now Rosie beamed. "That's right. Let's go up to the suite and sit down with Arianna."

Heidi sighed. Then she got up from the table. "You don't waste any time, do you?"

Rosie linked her arm with Heidi's. At last, one of the princesses was ready to head in the right direction. She could only hope that Arianna would feel the same way.

Chapter 7

"Hello? Arianna?" Rosie called out, pushing open the suite's heavy door. "It's Rosie and Heidi." The air was thick with silence.

"She's not here," Heidi said, quickly checking their bedroom. "Maybe she's back at the mixer."

Rosie shook her head. They'd both seen Arianna run off extremely upset. "I don't think she'd go back to the pool after what happened," she said slowly, trying to decide what to do. "She didn't look as if she wanted to be near anyone."

"But where else could she be?" Heidi asked nervously, playing with her rings.

"I have no idea," Rosie said. "But we'll find her. There are only so many places she can be." The truth was, Rosie was very, very worried. If Arianna wasn't at the mixer or in their suite . . . where was she?

Rosie and Heidi walked down the hallway toward the elevator bank. An elevator stopped on their floor. Rosie held her breath as the doors slid open. Could it be Arianna?

Out stepped Prince Joshua, a nice but rather bewildered-looking prince. He always was confused about something, and tonight was no exception.

"Oh, hello," he said, surprised to see them. "I think I got out on the wrong floor."

"You haven't seen Princess Arianna by any chance, have you?" Rosie asked. "We've been looking for her."

"Arianna, Arianna," he said, appearing to be deep in thought. "Short, blond hair, glasses?"

Heidi shook her head. "Tall, black hair, blue eyes."

"Don't think so. I'd have noticed a girl like that," he said with a wink. "Where are you two off to? I hear there's a mixer going on in the ballroom. Or maybe it's by the golf course. I was trying to find it when I ran into you."

Another elevator opened, and Rosie and Heidi hurried inside. "Follow us," Rosie told Joshua as he eagerly stepped in . . . and pressed the UP button.

"I have a terrible sense of direction," the prince confessed. "Most of the time, I end up just stumbling upon the very thing I'm trying to locate."

Rosie managed a weak smile. If only they could have the same kind of luck finding Princess Arianna.

Down by the pool, Carter was dancing amid

a big group of people, waving her arms in the air. She was having such a good time with Margret and Stephanie. She'd been afraid they wouldn't want to hang out with her without Rosie, but they didn't mind at all that she was the queen's assistant. But when she saw Rosie worriedly motioning to her, she said good-bye to her new friends and hurried over.

"Have you seen Arianna?" Rosie whispered urgently.

Carter shook her head. "I've been dancing, but . . . no. Haven't seen her." She grimaced. "Or heard her."

"I'm very concerned, Carter. No one seems to know where she is. Not the security officers, not the teachers, not anyone I've asked. Heidi is searching the lobby and restaurants right now with Prince Joshua."

"Where do you think she could be?" Carter asked. She didn't want to say what they both were thinking; that maybe something terrible had happened. She and Rosie had helped the P.P.P. enough to know that even princesses who least expected it could suddenly find themselves in grave danger.

Rosie started to shake her head, then stopped. "I—I don't know what to believe. Follow me." She walked quickly away from the crowd onto a deserted, flower-lined path that led to the hotel grounds.

To Carter's shock, Rosie took out a cell phone from her small satin purse. "We must call your father, Carter. He will know what to do."

Carter stared at the cell phone in Rosie's hand. "Where did that come from?" she said, flabbergasted. "I thought everyone had to turn them in when we arrived!"

"Executive privilege," Rosie replied, punching the speed-dial number for Mr.

Mason's cell. "And for once, I am very thankful to use it."

Unfortunately, Carter's father didn't answer his phone. Rosie left a short, urgent message for him to call her back as soon as possible.

"You know what I'm going to say," Carter told Rosie as she turned off the phone.

Rosie paced back and forth on the path. "How do we always end up in these situations, Carter?"

Carter shrugged. "We're good friends who care about people?" She put her hands on her hips. "Okay, we both know my father won't be happy if we take matters into our own hands . . . again. We can't tell the security staff and get everyone here in a panic. Just like at the homecoming dance, we don't have a choice," Carter finished, remembering how a dictator had almost succeeded in taking over Costa Luna. Without her help, Carter didn't know what would have happened to Rosie and her mother, Sophia.

"Arianna's safety comes first," Carter added.

"Arianna's safety comes first," Rosie repeated. She reached over and impulsively gave Carter a quick hug. "And that is why I know I have the best friend in the world."

"Where in the world has Arianna gone?" Carter wondered aloud. "It's not like she can call a limo to come and pick her up."

"When I need to be alone at the palace, there is a bench under a shady grove of mango trees that I visit," Rosie said.

Carter snapped her fingers. "Lake. Boathouse. Privacy."

Rosie nodded. "It's as good a place as any to start."

And the two friends ran off into the night.

Moonlight splashed over the top of the boathouse as the girls made their way down the winding path to the lake.

"It's kind of creepy here with no one around," Rosie whispered, glancing back over her shoulder.

"Everyone's at the mixer," Carter said. "Even all the security guards." The door to the boathouse was locked. The canoes and kayaks looked undisturbed.

"I thought she might have taken one of the boats out, but I guess not," Carter said, squinting at the water in the dark. An owl hooted somewhere in the woods.

Then, suddenly, Carter heard it. A branch cracked.

"Rosie!" she whispered. Rosie held up her hand and motioned for Carter to be quiet. Together they began to tiptoe around the corner of the boathouse. The sound could have been made by a deer or a raccoon or some other kind of animal—or perhaps a person. Arianna?

"Maybe this wasn't such a good idea," Rosie said under her breath, clutching Carter's arm. They cautiously crept forward. The owl hooted again, and Carter felt little beads of sweat breaking out on her forehead.

Suddenly, a blinding light shone directly in their faces.

"Ahhh!" Carter screamed, jumping back.

"Claire!" Rosie exclaimed. "What are you doing?"

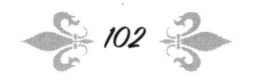

"I could ask you the same question," Claire said, turning her flashlight dimmer on. She wore a denim jacket over a tank top and a white skirt. "I lost my watch and thought it might have slipped off when I was kayaking today. I came down to see if I could find it, but no luck."

Carter exchanged a look with Rosie. She didn't really feel like letting her snobby suitemate in on what was going on, but at this point they needed all the help they could get. "I'm sorry you lost your watch, but we've lost something more important," Carter told her. "Arianna." She quickly filled her in on what had happened.

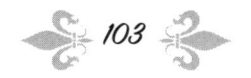

To Carter's surprise, Claire didn't make any wisecracks. Instead, she pulled a map of the hotel grounds out of her jacket pocket. "They close off certain areas of the resort at night. If Arianna is out here, she could only wander down three different paths. They all branch out from a central point, beyond the equestrian center." Claire tapped the map with her finger. "Why don't we head over there and split up? If we don't find her within fifteen minutes, we head back to our starting point."

"Okay," Carter said, wondering how Claire knew so much about the resort . . . and why all of a sudden she was so willing to help. Was she sending them on a wild goose chase?

Rosie nodded. "That sounds like as good a plan as any."

"If we don't find her, we need to go back to the hotel and report her missing." Claire looked grim. "A missing princess is no joke."

Carter felt the buffet snacks she'd eaten flop over in her stomach. She and Rosie knew more about missing princesses than probably anyone else at the summit. She didn't want to alarm anybody, but she'd just had a terrible thought. What if Heidi's country had finally had enough of the Silano family's trash talk?

What if Arianna had been kidnapped?

Chapter 8

"Arianna," Carter whispered, moving along the unlit wooded path. "Arianna!" At first, Carter, unnerved by the dark and the thought that maybe there were animals in the woods besides owls, had walked so quickly that she was practically jogging. She had slowed her pace now, calling out the princess's name every few feet.

She kept picturing her dad's reaction when he found out that Princess Arianna was missing. The story could go so many ways. The best-case scenario? Arianna was fine, Mr. Mason wasn't angry, and everyone went home happy. The worst-case scenario?

Arianna had run away or been kidnapped, Mr. Mason was furious, and everyone went home miserable.

Everyone but Arianna, because she was still missing.

"Best scenario. Definitely best scenario," Carter muttered as she walked further down the passageway.

She thought she would hear Rosie and Claire calling out Arianna's name, but the pathways all went in different directions. She couldn't even hear the DJ's music back at the mixer, and that was loud.

"I wish I was back there right now. We're missing the whole thing," Carter complained to the mosquitoes, lifting her hair off her hot, sticky neck. "All because of a princess."

There was a flash of heat lightning, and for a moment, Carter thought she was hallucinating. There, in the distance off the path, Carter saw something. Was it a person? Or wishful thinking? The sky lit up again, and this time Carter could see more clearly.

It was a person.

A girl.

She ran off the path and down a slight incline toward a cluster of oak trees.

"Arianna?" Carter called out tentatively at first, and then she was sure. "Arianna!"

Rosie's quarrelsome roommate was a wilted mess.

"Carter!" Arianna cried out, stumbling toward her and flinging clammy arms around her. "I've never been so glad to see anyone in my life. Even if it's you!"

"Thanks, I think," Carter said, pulling back to look at her. Tear-stained face, arms covered with dirt and sweat, disheveled hair, wrinkled party dress . . . it was almost as if the Princess Protection Program itself had appeared to de-princess the girl.

Arianna took gulps of air. "I'm sorry. That didn't come out how I meant it to. It's just that I've been wandering in the woods for an eternity. I was beginning to think I'd be out here all night!"

"How'd you get all the way out here, anyway?" Carter asked, gesturing to the trees.

Arianna swallowed. "Well, you heard what happened at the pool, right?"

Carter nodded. "Um, no offense, but . . . who didn't?"

"I didn't want to believe that what Margret was saying was true, but I guess in my heart I knew that she wasn't making it up." Arianna held up something small and shiny.

Carter stared. "Don't tell me you have a phone, too. I am so not following the rules next time."

Arianna kept talking. "I was walking

without thinking, you know? I was just so upset and so mad. I wanted to call my family back in Manchara to find out the truth, and I wanted to be alone when I did." Her voice cracked. "I was on the phone with my mother and my brother, and I wasn't paying attention to where I was going. I thought I was on one of the hotel's hiking trails. I didn't even realize where I was going because the conversation I was having with my family was so upsetting. And then when I clicked off, I was lost. And I'd been on the phone for so long that my battery had died, and I couldn't make another call."

Hearing Princess Arianna speak so candidly made Carter soften . . . a little. She could only imagine how hard it would be hearing that your home might be threatened and that your actions and behavior had been doing a lot more harm than good.

"Did talking to your family help?" she

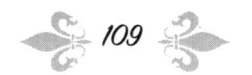

asked in what she hoped was a Rosie-like, caring way.

Arianna rubbed tiredly at her eyes. "No. Yes. I mean, what they said didn't exactly make me feel better. But it definitely was the wake-up call I needed."

"So are you saying you and Heidi—"

"We are never going to be best friends like you and Rosie. But I think we can manage to coexist without involving the United Nations."

Carter smiled. So much for her assistant act fooling anyone. "C'mon," she told Arianna, walking back up to the path. "There are some people who are going to be very happy to see you."

"So you're saying that nothing happened—no kidnappers, no animal attacks, nada," Claire said, handing Carter a bottle of icy cold water.

"Thanks," Carter said gratefully, dropping onto the couch next to Arianna. Once she and Arianna had met up with Rosie, the three girls had gone directly back to the suite.

Claire had been unusually nice, getting them water, cold washcloths—she'd even run down to the vending machine and come back with candy bars and bags of potato chips.

"Oh, good, they're here," Claire said now as someone rapped on the suite door.

"They?" Carter repeated, casting an inquisitive eye.

Claire walked over and let in . . . Mr. Mason and a woman in a dark pantsuit, her long hair pulled back in a low bun.

Carter gasped. "Dad!"

"That's the Director of the Princess Protection Program," Rosie whispered to Carter in surprise. "I haven't seen her in ages."

"Good work, Claire," Mr. Mason said, stepping inside and shaking her hand.

The Director's face was serious. "This could have blown up in our faces if not for your swift action."

Carter's jaw dropped. If her father and the Director of the P.P.P. were here and they knew Claire, that could only mean one thing. . . .

"You work for the P.P.P.?" Carter asked Claire, incredulous.

"How about a 'Hi, Dad. Nice to see you,'" her father said, coming over and sweeping Carter up in a hug.

"Sorry. Hi, Dad," Carter said, hugging him back.

"Major Mason, it is a surprise and a pleasure to see you," Rosie said, smiling brightly at Carter's father.

"I'm sorry I couldn't tell you sooner," Claire said, flashing a grin. "But it was for your own safety. I am part of a subset of the P.P.P. known as Divagate."

"English, please," Carter said.

Claire laughed. "My role this week was to be part of the summit's security staff—and my cover of a princess with a bad attitude was designed to help me feel people out and make sure everyone was safe."

"I knew you couldn't be as rude as you were acting," Rosie said, looking pleased.

"And *I* knew there was something unusual about you knowing the hotel grounds as well as you did," Carter said, shaking her head.

Claire laughed again. "I'm not an angel, but you're right, Rosalinda—my behavior was meant to illustrate how off-putting snobbish behavior from a royal is."

"So you aren't a royal after all?" Carter asked, making sure.

Claire shook her head. "My parents are both schoolteachers. I'm from Indiana."

The Director had taken a seat between Rosie and Arianna and was quietly talking with the princess.

"We've come to take Arianna and Heidi home," Mr. Mason told Carter. "Claire had already tipped us off, and your phone call came in while we were on our way here."

"See?" Carter said, raising her eyebrows. "I did call you."

Her father gave her a wry smile. "Duly noted. Heidi has already packed her things and is waiting with a representative from the P.P.P. in a car downstairs."

"Home?" Carter repeated, looking at the Director and then back to her father. If the Director was here, that meant the P.P.P. was involved. Carter had a pretty good feeling that Arianna wasn't going to be flying first class to Manchara.

Her father's expression told her that her hunch was correct.

"So we don't even get to say good-bye to her?" Carter asked.

"Once she's settled in you can give her a call," Mr. Mason assured her. "We want to give Manchara and Pengova a chance to work their troubles out, and keeping the princesses under our protection until that happens is best for all concerned."

The Director and Arianna had finished their conversation, and now Arianna had stood up. "Thanks, everybody. For everything. I—I really appreciate it."

"That is what friends are for," Rosie said kindly.

Arianna paused. "I know I haven't exactly been easy to live with. But I promise if we ever run into each other again, I'll be a different person."

"You can say that again," Carter mumbled as Arianna went into her bedroom with Claire to start packing. If the Princess

Protection Program was involved, Arianna would end up with a new name and a new home—at least temporarily. She hoped her dad wasn't getting any ideas. Having one "cousin from Iowa"—aka Rosie—had been more than enough.

"Have you had a good week at the summit?" Mr. Mason asked Rosie.

"Oh, yes, Major Mason," she said, her eyes shining. "It's been one of the best weeks of my life!"

Carter nodded. "Ditto."

Mr. Mason and the Director smiled. "Enjoy the rest of your stay here," the Director said. "Carter, Your Highness." And she walked out.

"You and me, pal," Mr. Mason said, holding out his hand for his traditional fist bump with Carter.

"You and us, Dad," Carter said, pulling a giggling Rosie over for a three-way bump back. She couldn't believe that tomorrow was their last day here.

Carter had to make sure Rosie and Prince Darius got to have some time together.

That's what *best* friends were for.

Chapter 9

"Say 'cheddar'!" Carter said the next morning, snapping a shot of Rosie with her arms around Margret and Stephanie. They were standing on a huge manicured grass lawn nestled in the shadows of the mountains.

"It's so nice!" Rosie said, looking at the picture in the camera screen. No tiaras, no ball gowns—just the faces of three happy girls in T-shirts and ponytails, looking like normal teenagers, not royalty.

Arianna and Heidi had left with Major Mason and the Director the night before, along with Claire. For the first time all week, Rosie had had a peaceful night's sleep. Of course, the quiet helped. But Rosie was also filled with happiness at the thought that her new friends would get the help they so desperately needed . . . and that their countries were on the road to reconciliation.

Rosie took some pictures with Carter's camera as the girls made crazy faces and bunny ears.

"I'll send them to you guys when I get back home," Carter promised the royals.

Rosie was reminded by her friend's words that today was the last day of the Prince and Princess Summit. Not that she needed reminding. Everywhere she looked, groups of new friends were hugging each other, taking pictures, and exchanging contact information. A seven-piece band was on the main patio, playing the national anthem of each country in attendance, and flags had been posted around the hotel grounds from each country.

Rosie proudly noticed the Costa Lunan flag whipping smartly in the wind. "This week went by so quickly," she said to her friends.

Princess Margret agreed. "We did get a lot accomplished, though. I can't wait to go home and tell my parents that I want to study communications *and* poli-sci in college!"

Princess Stephanie was busily typing in everyone's details on her PDA with a purple manicured fingernail. "We'll definitely meet up this summer," she told Rosie. "Maybe you and Carter can join our yacht trip to Italy in August. We've got room for thirty."

"Whoa," Carter said, widening her eyes.

"And our castle is always open," Princess Margret said graciously. *"Mi casa es su casa."* She waved to a prince who was heading toward the hotel. "Gotta run, girls. Charlie! Wait up!" she called, dashing off.

"Yeah, and I better get moving, too,"

Carter said, looking over at the table the living-green group was starting to set up. "We need all the volunteers we can get for our 'clean up the lakeshore' event this morning. You'd be amazed at the kind of things people have thrown in the water. Styrofoam, bottles . . . even a sink!"

Rosie and Carter said good-bye to Stephanie, and walked over to the table. "We thought it would be cool to give back to the community before we left," Carter explained. "The cleanup is going to take place off-property on the part of the lake that the hotel doesn't own. There'll be tons of security—the event wasn't publicized, so none of the locals will know about it until after everything is all clean and unpolluted."

"I love seeing ideas put into action," Rosie said, taking a pair of protective plastic gloves and a garbage bag. "I would be most happy to help clean up."

Darius and his friends walked over. They all wore neon green work vests over their shorts and T-shirts. "That's cool that you're helping out," the prince told Rosie. "Making a difference—that's what it's all about."

"The work goes faster if people work in pairs," Carter said nonchalantly. "Why don't you guys go together? I'm staying here to staff the table, make sure we don't run out of any of the cleaning supplies, show people the poison-ivy chart . . ."

"Cool," Darius said, shaking his friends' hands before they headed off with a group that was going to focus their efforts on a nearby creek. "Later, dudes." Then he turned to Rosie. "Ready to make a difference?"

She held up her gloved hands. "Trash, here we come."

"I'm sorry we didn't get to dance again last night," Darius said as they picked their way through a thicket of trees. Sunlight filtered through the branches, and birds hopped on the pine-needle–covered ground. "I heard what happened. Crazy, huh?"

"I'm sorry, too. And you are right; it *was* kind of crazy," Rosie agreed, stopping to pick up a gum wrapper and toss it in her trash bag. "But, really? I am glad things turned out the way they did for the princesses. Sometimes it takes something big to make people change their behavior."

"Margret said Arianna and Heidi left the summit with some sort of international rescue organization and that Claire was one of their escorts," Darius said.

Rosie gave a sort of half nod, half shrug. The less she divulged about the P.P.P., the better. "Arianna's and Heidi's families were quite distraught when they heard about their daughters' behavior."

Darius nodded. "Finally the feud may be

put to rest for good. And when I return home, I promise I will do what I can to make sure that harmony—not confrontation—is the name of the game."

He is such a good person, Rosie thought, wishing Darius lived in Costa Luna and not an ocean away. Smart, funny, caring . . . not to mention cute. I may have to use my private jet more often.

The prince hesitated for a moment, then stopped and held his finger up to his lips. "Shhh. Follow me."

Rosie walked as quietly as she could, stepping over branches, until the thicket opened up onto a wide expanse of grass. "Oh, wow," she said, staring. In front of them were three deer, their ears pointed. They stood motionless, looking at Rosie and Darius.

"How did you know they were here?" Rosie whispered.

"I saw the bigger one out of the corner of my eye, and usually if you see one deer, another isn't far away."

They watched the animals, who stood for a few seconds, and then loped off in the opposite direction, their white tails pointing up.

"What an easy life they lead," Rosie mused. "Their biggest worry is what tree to fall asleep under or where to find dinner in the forest."

"Our lives are a bit more complicated," Darius said with a laugh. "But I wouldn't trade our world for anything."

"We are very lucky," Rosie agreed. "I tell myself that every morning when I wake up."

"I love traveling and learning about the world," Darius said, sitting down on a fallen tree trunk. Rosie sat next to him. "I spent two weeks in Japan last year, and soon I'll be leaving for Australia on an official state visit with my father."

Rosie could relate. "Because I have only been queen for a short time, I wanted to hold off on taking too many official trips. I felt that I needed to get to know the ropes first. But I've already traveled to Washington, D.C., and some neighboring island nations, and there is a trip to the Middle East that I am quite looking forward to later in the year—after I visit Canada, England, and Chicago in the U.S.," she finished.

"Any chance you will be visiting the Riviera?" Darius asked, his brown eyes twinkling. "I would love to show you my country—the architecture, the land, the people."

"I might just have to add Ileos to my royal itinerary," Rosie said, surprising herself with her boldness. "It would be nice to see you again, Darius."

"Count on it," Darius told her. He

looked down at the ground, then moved his hand over, lacing his gloved fingers with hers. "It's been really cool to be here, around people who know exactly how we feel. A lot of the time people say they know how you feel, but there's no way they could."

"It is true," Rosie said, her hand feeling warm and secure in his. "Sometimes I feel a lot of pressure, but seeing that there are other teenagers like us going through similar things makes it easier to handle."

Darius looked up at her. The sun brought out warm golden flecks in his eyes, and the tip of his nose was a teeny bit sunburned. He swallowed. "I feel kind of stupid actually asking you this, but you are queen and all, and, well, would it be okay if I kissed you?"

Rosie felt a flush of red creep across her cheeks. "Hmmm. Well," she said slowly, hoping he couldn't hear the insanely loud thumping of her heart, "I think it would be acceptable."

And then the prince leaned over and gave her a sweet, soft kiss.

"I'm glad we got to see each other again," Darius said, pulling away and smiling. "And I hope we can see more of each other in the future."

"I hope so, too," Rosie said, smiling shyly.

"I think you're really cool, Rosie," Darius said quietly.

"You are, too," Rosie said. Darius was just so easy to talk to. It was as her mother always told her: people were just people, whether they were wearing a crown or a pair of work boots.

They worked for another hour, until they had a full bag of trash—old shoes, glass bottles, soggy fast-food bags—between them.

Darius hefted the bag over his shoulder as they headed back to the Dumpster that had been set up in the main area. "Let's get Carter to take a picture of us."

Rosie grimaced, looking down at herself. "Like this?"

He gave a firm nod. "I like it. We can change the image of what being a royal is all about," Darius said, and she realized he was serious. "Stuffy parties, etiquette, all the rules and regulations—I want to be known for doing stuff. Not just talking about it."

"This is the kind of press we want," Rosie said, warming to the idea. The prince was right. So what if she was covered with grass stains? A photograph of her and Darius showing how rewarding it was to get involved in a cleanup—muddy shoes and all—could persuade other people to do the same thing in their communities.

"The press loves to try and catch us

doing something foolish," Darius continued, "but this is what being a true leader is all about."

"But first?" Rosie said, coming to a stop. She gave him a mischievous grin. "There's one more thing I want to do before we get back to the summit."

"Your wish is my command, Your Highness," Darius teased back.

And Rosie leaned over and gave Prince Darius a kiss.

Being a queen definitely did have its privileges.

Chapter 10

"I'm such a traditionalist," Carter declared as the line of customers inched forward at the hotel's old-fashioned ice-cream parlor. The walls were lined with old movie posters, everything from *Gone with the Wind* to *Bedknobs and Broomsticks*. An Elvis Presley song played on the speakers, and decorative ceiling fans whirled above their heads.

When it was her turn, Carter smiled at the patient young man holding a scoop behind the counter. "I'll have a dish of vanilla, two scoops. With gummy bears, strawberries, and peanuts. Please."

"If that's traditional, I'd hate to see what

being adventurous would entail," Rosie said with a laugh, gazing at the choices on the menu before ordering a hot fudge sundae.

"Are you sure you don't mind staying here with me?" Carter asked after they got their order and searched for seats in the crowded and noisy dining area. They squeezed into two white chairs with yellow leather padded seats at a small wrought-iron table.

"Absolutely," Rosie insisted, smiling at her friend. Carter had asked her at least ten times if she wanted to hang out with Darius instead of with her, but Rosie was adamant. This was her last night at the summit—which meant it was her last chance to spend time with her best friend. And she couldn't think of anything more fun than getting ice cream and talking about the incredible time they'd had that week.

"So where do you think Arianna and

Heidi are?" Carter said, dipping her spoon into her ice cream.

"Definitely not together," Rosie said, swallowing a spoonful of hot fudge. "They could be anywhere, really. The Princess Protection Program has ties all around the world."

"My dad probably knows," Carter said. "But he'll never spill the beans. He's very professional."

"I'm so glad he let you join me, Carter," Rosie told her. "Wasn't the summit fun?" She was already looking ahead to the next one four years from now.

"Totally. You royals really know how to work hard and play hard." Carter nibbled a green gummy bear head. "Although I would like to find out where we are." She waggled her spoon in the air. "You're sure you don't know?"

Rosie smiled. "I would rather not find

out. This way, it is like a magical place that we can only return to in our memories."

Carter stared at her. "That was very deep, Rosie." She scraped the bottom of her parfait glass. "Almost as deep as this dish of ice cream, which, by the way, is amazing."

"I bet you are looking forward to getting back to the cabin, and to your life in Louisiana," Rosie said, feeling a tiny tinge of envy. She had only lived with Carter and her father for a short while, but it was long enough to see how much they really cared about each other. And the lakeside cabin where they lived had to be one of the most beautiful places on Earth.

"My friends and some classes at school, yeah," Carter admitted. "My dad, sort of. The bait buckets? Um, not so much."

"That's what keeps life interesting," Rosie stated firmly. "Without true lows, we would not know the joys of real highs."

"And you know what else keeps things interesting?" Carter asked, leaning forward and resting her elbows on the table. "Cute boys."

"I couldn't agree more," Rosie said, her eyes twinkling. Darius and his friends had just ordered cones and shakes, and when he spotted Rosie, she waved them over.

"We were just talking about you," Darius said, grinning at Rosie. "We need your help."

"Really?" Rosie said, happy to see him. She had a feeling that his "running into her" wasn't exactly a coincidence. Not that she had a problem with that. It felt really good to have a guy she liked like her back—and know that it wasn't because she was a queen. Darius liked her for her.

"Terrible argument. Brutal. We decided that only someone who knows what it is like to rule a country could have the skill to resolve it," Darius said somberly, his right dimple twitching as he took a sip of his milk shake.

His friend, Prince Gordon, licked his chocolate cone. "Very serious debate we were having about the best arcade game of all time. Is it a racing game . . . or a flight game?"

"Or is it the tried-and-true classic, pinball?" Darius asked, pretending to pull back an imaginary ball shooter and push the flippers.

Prince Eduard smiled apologetically at the girls. "It does help when you have your own arcade. Even if it's in your mind."

Carter held up her palms. "Sorry, boys, but it's no contest. I was practically raised with a game controller in my hand. I know you guys are royals and all, and so I wouldn't want to embarrass you, but I think we need a play-off. Because not only is HipHopTwirlrrr the best arcade game ever—I can beat all of you with my eyes closed."

"She's serious," Prince Gordon said, raising an eyebrow.

"I can vouch for Carter's expertise," Rosie told them in a grave voice. "And I must be honest—I am no stranger to blinking lights, beeping noises, and small creatures fighting for power."

Prince Darius sighed. "There's only one thing we can do, then. Challenge you ladies to a full-on battle in the hotel's video arcade."

"If you're up for it," Prince Eduard said.

"If you dare," Prince Gordon added.

Rosie and Carter looked at each other, and then, at exactly the same time, dropped their spoons into their parfait glasses.

"Game on, boys," Rosie said, standing up. "If we win, we fly home via private jet, you fly commercial. With no music, video games, or pillows."

"*If* we win? They are going down," Carter said gleefully, shaking her head at the mental image.

"I hope you like cramped legroom," Gordon said coolly to Carter, taking a crunchy bite of his waffle cone.

"And if we win? I'm thinking weekly press releases touting our charm, good looks, and athletic ability," Darius came back as the princes low-fived him.

Rosie looked around the ice-cream parlor at her laughing friends and squeezed her eyes shut, trying to freeze a picture of this night in her memory for always.

"Ah, thinking about losing already, Rosie?" Darius teased as he took Rosie's hand and the group walked out of the ice-cream parlor toward the arcade.

"Oh, no," Rosie told him, giving the

prince a playful shove in the ribs. "Just trying to imagine how a bunch of experts like you will explain away your overwhelming and crushing defeat."

"Ah, I see how you operate," Darius said. "Beautiful on the outside, lethal on the inside."

"You know what they say," Rosie told him. "All's fair in love and gaming."

Carter leaned over. "You know we are going to beat the royal trousers off them, right?" she whispered as they walked. "HipHopTwirlrrr is the most intense game ever. And I've played it a million times. We will show them no mercy."

Rosie put her free arm around Carter's waist. They would beat the boys—she had no doubt.

But she also had no doubt that Darius—even though she suspected he was quite competitive—wouldn't really mind.

Darius let out a long, exaggerated sigh as they walked into the arcade. "I really like you Rosie, but if we're competitors, I've got to say it. Get ready to lose, Your Highness."

Carter gave Rosie a fist bump and went to get tokens with Eduard. "Let's show 'em how it's done, Rosie," she called over her shoulder.

Okay, maybe the prince was a teensy bit more aggressive than she had originally thought.

But that was okay. She respected people who went after what they wanted. And Rosie knew how to smooth things over when the outcome wasn't quite what they anticipated.

After all, she was the queen.